3 4028 08218 8468
HARRIS COUNTY PUBLIC LIBRARY

W9-AMO-623

$17.95
ocn822959255
06/21/2013

DISCARD

Polly's
pirate party

No Bath, No Cake!

Polly's Pirate Party

Copyright © 2012 by NordSüd Verlag AG, CH-8005 Zürich, Switzerland.
First published in Switzerland under the title *Pollys Piratenparty*.
English text copyright © 2013 by NorthSouth Books Inc., New York 10016.
Translated by David Henry Wilson.

All rights reserved.
No part of this book may be reproduced or utilized in any form or by any means, electronic or mechanical, including photo-copying, recording, or any information storage and retrieval system, without permission in writing from the publisher.

First published in the United States, Great Britain, Canada, Australia, and New Zealand in 2013 by NorthSouth Books, Inc., an imprint of NordSüd Verlag AG, CH-8005 Zürich, Switzerland.

Distributed in the United States by NorthSouth Books Inc., New York 10016.
Library of Congress Cataloging-in-Publication Data is available.
ISBN: 978-0-7358-4112-3 (trade edition).
Printed in Germany by Offizin Andersen Nexö Leipzig GmbH, 04442 Zwenkau, January 2013.

1 3 5 7 9 · 10 8 6 4 2
www.northsouth.com

FSC
www.fsc.org
MIX
Paper from
responsible sources
FSC® C012425

Matthias Weinert

No Bath, No Cake!

Polly's Pirate Party

$\mathcal{E}$arly one morning, just as the sun was peeping over the horizon,
something sailed through the mail slot on the good ship *Mary Anne* . . .

. . . and Pete, the pirate parrot, woke up with a start.

Pirate Captain Brummel and his crew leaped out of their hammocks and immediately grabbed hold of their weapons.

"What's happened?" they shouted in a panic.

"A letter came through the mail slot," said Pete, which was the absolute truth.

"A letter? Wow! I wonder what it says?" Very carefully, Captain Brummel opened the envelope.

"We've been invited to a birthday party!"
"Yippee!" Everyone was happy.

"A birthday party!" laughed Spoonbelly.
"So there's bound to be some cake!"

"And gummy bears too!" cried Tiny Tom.

"And fizzy drinks!"
cheered Hairpin Harry.

"Then we shall go!"
announced Captain
Brummel.

"Hip, hip, hooray!" and "Yahoo!" they shouted as they all rushed to set sail.

All except Pete. He had a serious expression on his face.

"Is that how you think you can go to a birthday party?" he asked. "Just look at your feet!"

"Eh? What's wrong with our feet?" asked Captain Brummel.

"They're filthy dirty," answered Pete, "like the rest of you!"

"So what?"

"You can't go to a birthday party with dirty feet!" said Pete, wagging his forefeather.

"Before you go, you must all have a bath."

"A bath?" howled Hairpin Harry. "A bath?" moaned Spoonbelly. "A bath?" groaned Tiny Tom. "No, no, anything but that!" pleaded Captain Brummel.

But Pete wouldn't budge.

"No bath, no cake!"

With more moans and groans, one by one the pirates got into the old wooden tub. They rubbed and they scrubbed until they were clean from top to toe. "And don't forget to comb your hair!" commanded Pete.

Half an hour later every man stood on the upper deck, fresh and fragrant, tidy and trim. Pete went from one to the other, inspecting feet and fingernails, ears and hair. "Very good, very good!" he commented approvingly.

"Hip, hip, hooray, we're on our way!" they cried,
hugging one another with joy.
But Pete shook his head. "I'm afraid not," he said.

"Your clothes may be all right for pirating, but there's no way you can wear them to a birthday party!" declared Pete. "If you're invited to a party, you have to wear something smart."

"But we don't want to wear something smart!" protested Captain Brummel.

"No smarty, ☠
no party!" said Pete.

And so all the men made their way
down the gangplank . . .

. . . and across the town . . .

. . . straight to George's Gorgeous Fashions.

There they were measured and modeled . . .

. . . and when they left
George's Gorgeous an hour later,
they looked like a million dollars in
their smart new clothes.

"So now we can go!" said Captain Brummel with a grin on his face.

They all nodded in vigorous agreement. All except Pete.

"There's just one teeny-weeny detail," he said. "You need to take a present."

"A present?" cried Tiny Tom. "A present?" echoed Hairpin Harry. "A present?" re-echoed Captain Brummel.

"I may have an idea," said Spoonbelly.

"How about a saber? You can give someone a lovely poke in the bottom with that," he suggested.

"Or a rope. You can tie someone up like a boa constrictor," proposed Hairpin Harry.

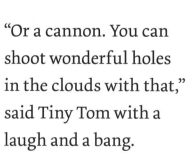

"Or a wooden leg. It might come in handy one day," said Captain Brummel enthusiastically.

"Or a cannon. You can shoot wonderful holes in the clouds with that," said Tiny Tom with a laugh and a bang.

"Stop!" cried Pete, who was getting fed up with all these stupid ideas.
"Saber, rope, wooden leg, cannon—those aren't presents for a little girl!"

"So what is a present for a little girl?" asked Captain Brummel.
"A doll! She can take it in her arms, and hold it and cuddle it," said Pete.
"So as far as I'm concerned, no doll, no cake."

The men all went down the gangplank . . .

. . . and across the town to Tiptop's Toy Shop.

Back on board again, they proudly showed Pete what they had bought.

"Very good, very good," said Pete approvingly. "Now all you have to do is wrap the present."

"Wrap?" asked the pirates.

"Wrap. Presents need to be wrapped in wrapping paper," explained Pete.
"You did buy some wrapping paper, didn't you?"

Half an hour later, Captain Brummel and his men returned. Pete inspected the wrapped present.

Without a word, he walked up and down the deck. Each man held his breath.

After half an eternity, Pete cleared his throat and finally uttered the words of liberation: "You can go now."

There were wild celebrations on board. Hurray! They'd done it!
Now nothing could go wrong.

Barely ten minutes later, the *Mary Anne* reached No. 12 Lavender Lane.

The mouths of the pirates began to water as soon as they saw the freshly baked birthday cake.

HAPPY BIRTHDAY TO YOU

"Who are you?" asked Polly.

"I am Captain Brummel, and this is my crew. You invited us,"
answered Captain Brummel.

"Are you supposed to be pirates?" asked Polly with a look of disbelief on her face. "Of course," said Captain Brummel. "And now we want some cake."

"But you don't look at all like pirates!" said Polly. "Pirates have dirty feet, filthy clothes, and shaggy hair."

"Whereas you just . . .　　　　　　　　　look stupid!"

"So as far as I'm concerned:

"No pirates, no cake!"

And Polly slammed the front door . . .

. . . but a moment later she opened it again.

"You can keep your silly doll! I wanted a cannon, or a saber, or a wooden leg, or at least a rope to tie someone up with!"

Then Polly slammed the door again, and the pirates trudged slowly back to the ship.

"Back already?"

And so it was a wonderful birthday party after all . . .

. . . and they had tons and tons of cake.

Harris County Public Library
Houston, Texas

DISCARD